Unlucky

Unlucky

Signs and superstitions
from around the world

Megan McKean

Hardie Grant

BOOKS

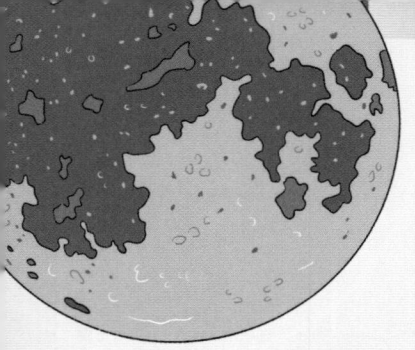

Contents

Introduction

Superstition is described as a widely held but irrational belief in supernatural influences, often linked to good or bad luck. It finds its way into many daily practices across various cultures. Rooted in tradition and folklore, superstitions have led to countless symbols and rituals meant to protect against misfortune and bring good luck and personal safety.

These practices offer a sense of security and control, providing comfort through rituals like wearing lucky clothing, carrying charms or avoiding certain numbers – all aimed at making the believer feel safe as they go about their every day. Adopting superstitions can affect an individual's choices, for better or worse, so you best keep your fingers crossed these rituals bring good fortune.

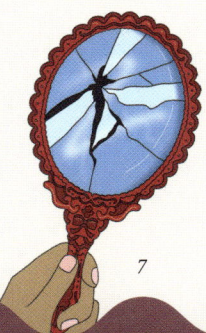

Bad Things Come in Threes

3

This is a superstition you can count on!

Three is a prevalent number in folklore, mythology, religion and literature – even fairytales frequently feature it: three magic wishes, three bears and three little pigs. The third time is the charm, yet one of the most enduring beliefs is that bad luck also comes in sets of three. Accidents, deaths or general misfortune are frequently thought to occur in threes.

While the true origin of this concept is unknown, psychologists suggest it persists due to the brain's pattern recognition and innate desire for certainty. Putting the limit of three on misfortunes brings comfort, as the streak of bad luck becomes finite.

Bananas on Ships

An *a-peeling* superstition for sailors to follow is to believe that bananas on ships are bad luck. Emerging in the 1700s, the story goes that when trade ships sailing the seas from the Caribbean and Spain would disappear, only the yellow fruits would be found, bobbing in the water among the wreckages. Blaming bananas for the ships' misfortune meant they soon became a bad omen, banned from being carried onboard.

The banana ban is still implemented on many boats and cruise ships today. Whether ripe or rotten, it's an omen not worth the risk for many seafarers!

Barbary Macaque

There's no monkeying around when it comes to the Barbary macaque in the British territory of Gibraltar. Home to several groups of these macaques, legend has it that if they were to ever leave Gibraltar, it would herald the end of British rule.

For many years, the British military cared for the macaques, with their protection formalised in 1913. Their belief in the monkeys was so important that when the macaque population fell during World War II, Prime Minister Winston Churchill issued a directive that their numbers were never to fall below twenty-four.

Bells on a Wedding Day

Ding-dong! Can you hear those wedding bells ring?
The ringing of bells during a wedding ceremony is a
Celtic tradition, rooted in the belief that their chimes
ward off evil spirits. Bells remain an important part
of Irish wedding customs, with some brides even
carrying small bells in their bouquets as they head
down the aisle for a little extra luck on the big day.

Bells are still a popular symbol of marriage,
and will often ring after a church ceremony to
celebrate the union of a newly wedded couple.

Bird Tapping on a Window

Whether bringing good news or bad,
this might ruffle some feathers.

Throughout the ages, people from many cultures
have believed birds to be messengers, winging their
way through the skies to deliver news. White birds
were often thought to bring positive change, while
black birds were seen as harbingers of death.

A bird tapping on your window could signal bad
luck, or could be a loved one trying to reach out
from another realm. On the other hand, a bird flying
into the glass could be a sign of good luck – though
maybe not for the bird.

Black Cat

'If a black cat crosses your path, bad luck is sure to follow' – a superstition that is not *kitten* around!

In the Middle Ages, as Christianity spread across Europe, cats became associated with witchcraft and paganism, with some myths claiming black cats were witches in disguise. In 1233, the Pope even declared cats to be instruments of Satan, with black cats being particularly Luciferian.

However, not everyone throughout the world considers black cats to be unlucky. In Japan, owning a black cat is thought to attract suitors to single women, while in Russia, black cats are a symbol of prosperity.

Break a Leg

'Break a leg!' is perhaps the only time you can cheerfully wish misfortune on someone; it is a unique case where saying 'good luck' is actually considered bad luck. Though the phrase is now a dead metaphor, it's a theatre superstition still very much alive today, used exclusively to wish performers well before they go on stage.

The phrase is thought to have originated in the early days of theatre, when ensemble actors would wait in the wings of the stage behind a 'leg line' to keep out of sight from the audience. If an actor 'broke' the leg line, they would be called on stage to perform, earning them a paycheck for that show.

Broken Mirror

Here's a superstition to reflect on: breaking a mirror results in seven years of bad luck.

Mirrors were highly prized by the ancient Romans because they believed mirrors reflected people's souls. Damaging a mirror was thought to damage the soul itself, an act so disrespectful that it would provoke the gods to rain bad luck on the person responsible.

However, all hope is not shattered. The Romans believed that both the body and soul renewed every seven years. While seven years is a lot of bad luck to endure, once the cycle ends, the soul is restored, and with it, so is the luck.

Broom Touching Feet

Beliefs to brush up on!

In Malaysia, it's thought that a broom should never touch the floor when not in use, as doing so may sweep away the household's luck. Brooms should also never be stacked together, as this is thought to lead to quarrels within the family.

Bringing an old broom into a new house is said to bring bad energy from the previous home. Additionally, touching someone's feet while sweeping is considered unlucky, and to dodge the bad luck, the broom needs to be spat on!

Cats Gossiping

In Dutch folklore, cats were suspected of being
terrible gossips. It was believed that secrets
should never be shared if a cat was in the room,
as the cat would spread the news throughout
the town.

Today, in the Netherlands, some people avoid
having important or private conversations
if their pet cat is nearby ... just in case.
Talk about catty behaviour!

Cheers with a Glass of Water

Cheers to health, wealth and happiness – but make sure your glass is full of champagne!

Clinking glasses filled with water is frowned upon in many cultures, with some believing that the act will bring bad luck or even death to the person you're raising a glass to. The US military goes as far as forbidding toasts with water. Naval folklore, in particular, claims that toasting with water will lead to death by drowning.

Chopsticks Standing Upright

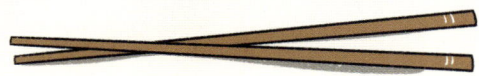

In many Asian cultures, placing chopsticks
upright is not only considered bad luck,
but also downright rude.

A pair of chopsticks sticking straight up from
a bowl of rice resembles incense sticking out of
ash-filled burners in funeral offerings, which is
viewed as a bad omen and disrespectful to the
dead. Beliefs abound that those who eat rice
with chopsticks placed upright will fall ill. In some
traditions, standing the chopsticks upright is even
seen as an invitation for spirits to dine with you –
and while these ghostly guests wouldn't eat
much, they would bring misfortune.

Clock as a Gift

This belief has stood the test of time.

In Chinese culture, giving a clock as
a gift is considered a very bad omen.
The Cantonese word for clock sounds
like the word for 'to die' or 'to end',
making it a symbol of time running out.
As a result, giving a clock as a gift is
associated with death and funerals,
and some even view it as a curse.

Commenting on a Cute Baby

In Thailand, calling a newborn baby ugly is not only accepted, but also encouraged. Many Thai people believe that babies are vulnerable to being stolen by evil spirits, with some thinking that the cuter the baby, the higher the likelihood of them being spirited away.

As a preventative measure, new parents will give their children ugly monikers and nicknames to confuse the spirits.

Corner Table

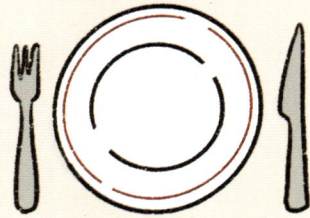

If you're looking for love, don't sit in the corner seat. A belief passed down through generations in Russia, Poland, Hungary and Ukraine warns single people against sitting at the corner of a table, as it is thought to mean they would never marry.

Corners can symbolise conflict, where two sides meet, and sitting in one could be seen to invite misfortune.

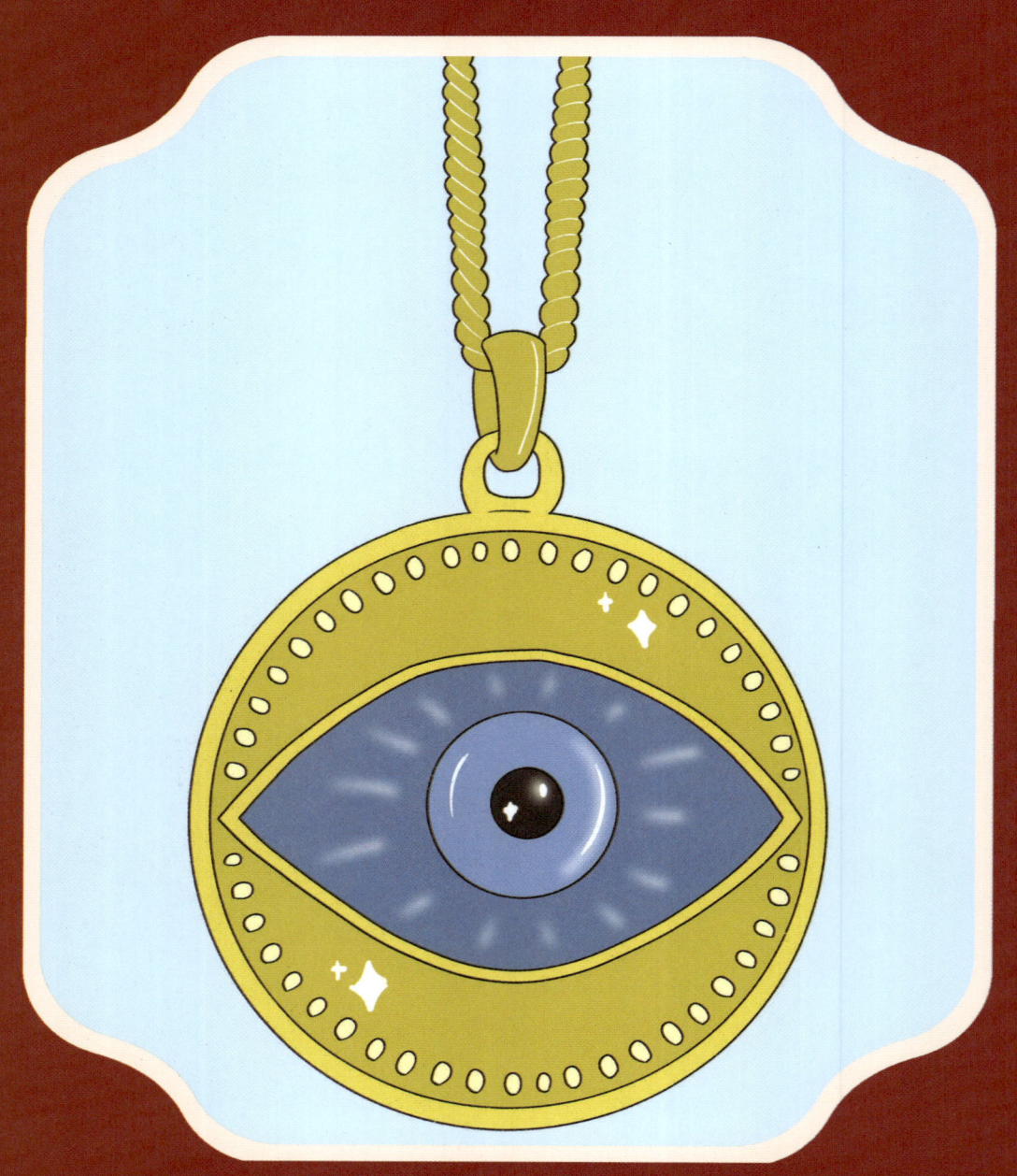

Evil Eye

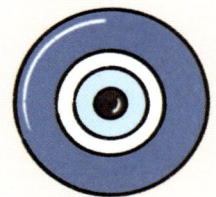

The evil eye is a supernatural belief in a curse cast by the malicious glare of someone wishing misfortune on another, usually driven by envy. Existing since prehistory, it is one of the most common superstitions across the world. Different cultures employ different measures for protection, with various charms, amulets and motifs used to shield against its harmful effects.

The evil eye talisman is traditionally designed in the shape of an eye, and is often blue or green, colours believed to foster spiritual protection and to shield against evil. Commonly worn as jewellery or a small accessory, it not only wards off negative energy but is also thought to bring good luck to the wearer.

Fingers Crossed

Perhaps the simplest superstition for wishing for a little extra luck is crossing your fingers. Originally, this gesture required two participants: they would touch their thumbs and cross their index fingers. The act was thought to mark an intersection of good spirits, anchoring a wish in place until it could come true.

Over time it became acceptable to make the gesture on your own. Early Christians crossed their index and middle fingers to resemble a physical cross, invoking the power of Christ for protection when faced with evil.

Flipping over Cooked Fish

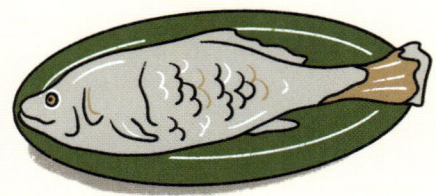

Never flipping over a cooked fish is such
a well-known and well-followed superstition in
China that there is no need to *carp* on about it.

Originating from coastal areas and fishing regions
in China, the belief is that a whole fish served
on a plate should never be turned over; the fish
symbolises a boat, and to flip over the cooked
fish means that you've capsized the fishing boat,
which will bring bad luck.

Full Moon

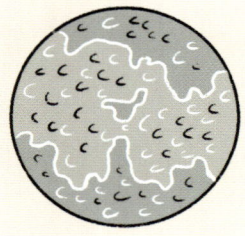

People who lived in ancient civilisations revered the moon as a deity, attributing powerful influences to its phases. The Roman goddess of the moon, Luna, was said to ride her silver chariot across the sky each night. This is where the word 'lunatic' comes from, as it was believed that the moon could affect mental health.

Today, people in many cultures still have a constellation of things to avoid during a full moon. From signing major contracts to having surgery or simply getting a haircut, plenty of people think the full moon sends normalcy into orbit and prefer to play it safe.

Haint Blue

Paint the town ... blue? In the early nineteenth century, homes in the southern United States often featured porch ceilings painted 'haint blue', a pale blue-green hue derived from crushed indigo plants. The word 'haint', a variation of 'haunt', referred to ghosts in African-American vernacular. It was believed that the colour would ward haints away from the home, as the blue ceiling was intended to mimic the sky and trick the ghost into passing through. The colour could also be seen to give the appearance of water, which ghosts could not cross.

While the superstitious significance of haint blue is no longer as strong, today it's believed the colour is a spider and wasp deterrent, with many homeowners still opting to paint their porch the signature shade.

In Bocca al Lupo

'Into the wolf's mouth!'; 'May it die!' – a dramatic way to wish an actor well, but what else would you expect from performers? This Italian idiom originated in opera and theatre as a way to wish good luck before a performance. Similar to the English saying, 'Break a leg!', this theatrical superstition holds that wishing someone good luck directly is actually bad luck. The response, *crepi*, means 'may it die', symbolising hope that the performance will go well.

The phrase originated from hunters who would embolden each other by using the superstitious negative phrasing to wish good luck, wolves and all.

Keys on the Table

A Swedish superstition still widely followed
today is keeping keys off the kitchen table
to prevent bad luck.

Unlocking the mystery behind the myth, it's said
that in the past, ladies of the night would signal
their availability by placing their keys on a hotel
or bar table. Parents would warn their daughters
that putting keys on the table could bring
misfortune – and risk someone mistaking
their intentions.

Knitting Outdoors

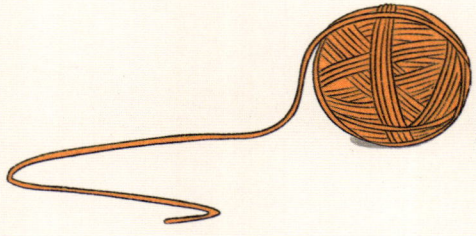

Knit one, purl two ... but keep it indoors! In Iceland, it's believed that knitting outdoors in late winter can prolong the cold days.

Many superstitions – and *purls* of wisdom – are woven through the knitting community, including the belief that bad luck will befall a knitter who leaves a project unfinished and the practice of knitting a strand of hair into an item to bind the recipient to the maker. The most common belief is the 'sweater curse', where giving a handmade sweater to a lover is said to lead to the recipient breaking up with the knitter – sometimes even before the sweater is completed!

Knock on Wood

Touching, tapping or saying 'knock on wood' is an apotropaic superstition meant to avoid 'tempting fate' after making a favourable prediction. Apotropaic magic is a type of protective magic, intended to ward off evil and deflect misfortune. While amulets and good luck charms are common, hand gestures like crossing fingers or touching wood also serve this purpose.

The true origins of the gesture are unknown, but one theory suggests it dates back to ancient pagan times when people believed that spirits lived in trees. By touching or knocking on the tree, they hoped to gain protection from bad luck.

Lemon and Chillies

To squeeze out as much good fortune as possible, try hanging a lemon by your front door!

In India, it's believed that hanging a lemon and chillies outside your home or store wards off the evil eye, as the combination of the fruits creates a protective charm. Some also believe this practice appeases Alakshmi, the Hindu goddess of misery and bad luck, and prevents her from entering the house.

This popular custom has even extended to vehicles, with small arrangements often seen hanging from car bumpers.

Macbeth

Toil and trouble will surely find you should you dare speak the name of Shakespeare's *Macbeth* inside a theatre.

According to theatrical superstition, uttering 'Macbeth' – unless while rehearsing or performing – will cause disaster, so it's typically referred to as 'The Scottish Play' instead. It's said that a coven of witches cursed the play after Shakespeare used a real spell in the script.

Today, should 'Macbeth' be spoken out of turn, a cleansing ritual must be performed to lift the curse. This may involve turning three times, spitting over the shoulder, or reciting a line from another Shakespeare play, with the hope that 'fair thoughts and happy hours' shall attend on you once again.

Magpie

'One for sorrow, Two for mirth,
Three for a funeral, Four for a birth ...'

In British superstition, a magpie is seen as nature's
fortune teller; the old rhyme attributes a different
fate to the number of magpies spotted.

To ward off bad luck from seeing a lone magpie,
it's customary to say 'Good morning, Mr Magpie, how
is your lady wife today?' Since magpies mate for life,
this greeting assumes the bird is most likely part of
a couple, turning the encounter into a good omen.

Manhole Cover

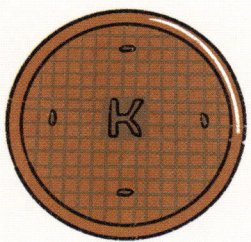

You'll have your lucky options well-covered with this superstition from Sweden, where manhole covers in the city streets bear different letters stamped in the centre. K stands for *källvatten* (freshwater) and is considered lucky, while an A for *avlopp* (sewage) is thought to bring bad fortune.

Standing on a K cover will bring *kärlek* (love), especially if you think of someone special. For extra luck, some believe jumping up on the cover multiple times will bring even more benefits.

Number Four

One, two, three, four – is there
a number feared more?

Tetraphobia, the irrational fear of the number four,
is a superstition common in East Asian cultures.
In many Asian languages, the word for 'four'
sounds similar to the word for 'death', giving
the number a negative connotation.

It's even speculated that the reason China did not
pursue a bid for the 2004 Olympic Games (after
losing the bid to host in 2000) was due to the
unpopularity of the number four. Instead, Beijing
waited a further four years to eventually host
in 2008 – a year tied to the auspicious number
eight in Chinese culture.

Owl

The owl has been the subject of superstition for people across many cultures and centuries, as both a positive and negative omen.

The ancient Greeks and Romans thought owls to be the messengers of witches; their unique hooting call a warning for an approaching witch. The bird is also viewed as ominous in India, where it's thought that if an owl screeches in front of a house, someone in the family will soon die.

Conversely, people in some other cultures see owls as a symbol of protection, such as in China where placing owl effigies on rooftops is thought to protect the home from lightning strikes. For some Native American people, owl poop is a sign of prosperity; a magnet for good luck.

Penny for Receiving Something Sharp

Want your gift to be a cut above the rest? There are rules to follow when gifting something sharp.

It's thought that gifting a knife can cause the relationship between the giver and recipient to be severed. To prevent this, the recipient should give payment; often the giver tapes a small coin to the blade of the knife for the receiver to return to them as 'payment'.

This superstition has been linked to the Vikings, who believed that gifting a knife implied the receiver couldn't purchase a quality knife of their own. To avoid the implication, Vikings would 'sell' a knife for the cost of one copper coin.

Purse on the Floor

'A purse on the floor is money out the door.'

According to Chinese culture, it's bad feng shui to place a handbag on the floor. As people usually carry important personal items in their bag, such as credit cards and money, to place it on the floor is disrespectful, and shows a disregard for money and wealth. People in many other cultures also follow this superstition, with Brazilians believing that if a person puts their wallet or bag on the floor, they will lose all their money.

Rat

Rats get the blame for a lot of negative moments in history: spreading disease, ruining food supplies and, in some cultures, foreshadowing death.
In Celtic mythology, a rat mass exodus meant a ship was going to wreck, and seeing a rat in a sieve could signify death – specifically of a family member away at sea.

On the Isle of Man, a modern superstition has emerged, where it is bad luck to use the word 'rat'. In its place, 'longtail' is the euphemism used.

Raven

Featured in many plays, poems and art throughout history, the raven is often depicted as an omen that can bring bad luck or even death.

Norse mythology has stories of two raven helpers who served the god Odin as his spies, while many stories of the Indigenous peoples of the Pacific northwest coast portray the raven as a trickster and a thief.

Raven superstitions persist today, with the Tower of London being home to at least six ravens at all times. Legend states that the British monarchy and the Tower will fall if the resident ravens ever leave their fortress.

Red Sunrise

'Red sky at night, sailors delight; Red sky at morning, sailors take warning' is a well-known nautical saying, repeated over the centuries. It's used as a simple rule of thumb for weather forecasting based on the reddish glow in the morning or evening skies.

A crimson sunrise is regarded as ominous, heralding an approaching storm – a warning to be prepared for an unpredictable and possibly dangerous day ahead.

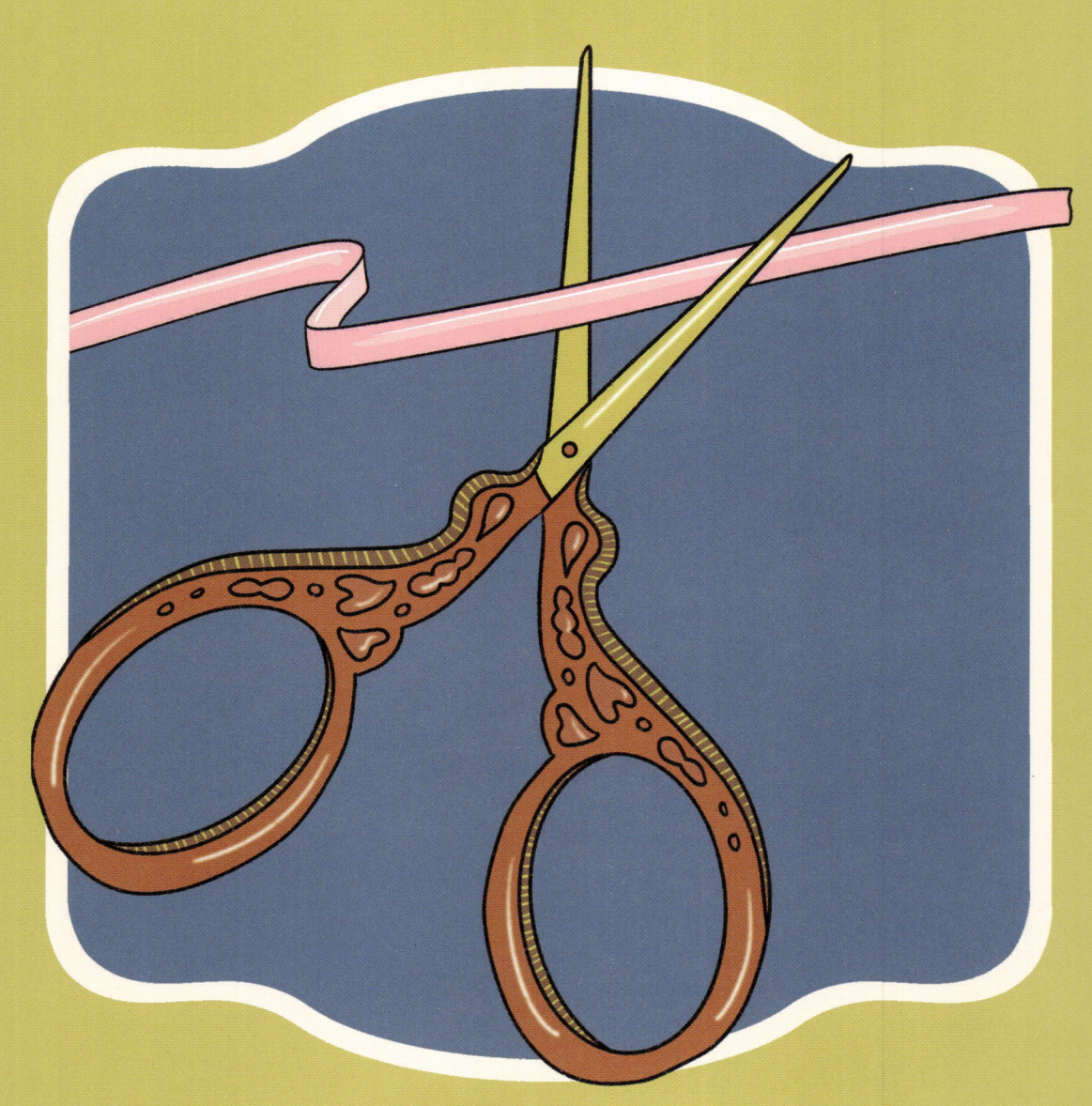

Scissors

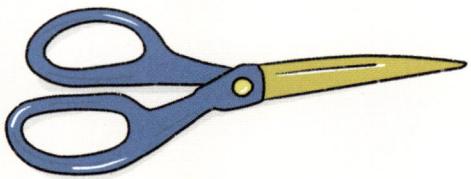

In Egypt, opening and closing scissors without cutting anything is taboo, as it's believed to cut through airborne evil spirits, angering them. In some cultures, dropping a pair of scissors is considered unlucky, even to the extent that it might cause a lover to be unfaithful – shear bad luck!

People in other cultures associate scissors with good fortune, using them as charms for protection against evil or to cut off bad energy. In Japan, placing scissors under a pillow is thought to prevent nightmares, while in Turkey, they are used to ward off the evil eye.

Shaking Hands across a Threshold

This is an unlucky omen to shake on.

In Russian folklore, a house spirit is believed to reside in the threshold, which is the space between two rooms. To bridge the gap in the doorway – either by shaking hands or greeting a guest with a kiss – is considered extremely bad luck, potentially inviting negative energy or signalling a break in the relationship. Still a widely practiced superstition today, one should wait until fully inside a Russian home before shaking hands.

Shoes on the Table

Is this bad luck or just bad manners? It's said that placing shoes on a table is unlucky, body and *sole*.

This belief is common in the north of England and is linked to coal mining. When a miner died in a colliery accident, their shoes would be placed on the table as a mark of respect. By extension, doing so outside this context came to be seen as tempting fate or as disrespectful to the dead.

Sleeping Direction

Waking up on the wrong side of the bed is more than just a metaphor for a ruined day; in feng shui, the right side of the bed is considered unlucky, while the left side is linked to good health, money and power.

In Japan, sleeping with your head facing north is considered a bad omen, as it mirrors the traditional direction in which the dead are buried. According to Vastu Shastra, the traditional Hindu system of architecture, your head should face east while sleeping to harness positive energy from the sun.

Whatever your beliefs, these are rituals you can follow with your eyes closed!

Spilling Salt

Perhaps this superstition should be taken
with a grain of salt?

Once a valuable commodity, salt played a vital role in the
preservation of food and was even treated as currency.
The economic importance of salt meant that spilling it
was wasteful and thought to surely bring misfortune.
Even Leonardo da Vinci's *The Last Supper* depicts Judas
knocking over the salt cellar, immortalising spilled
salt as unlucky.

Whether you believe it wholeheartedly – or maybe
just a sprinkle – to counteract the bad luck caused
by spilling salt, throw a pinch of the spilled grains over
your left shoulder and this should blind any evil spirits
lurking behind you.

Stepping on a Crack

'Step on a crack, break your mother's back' is a popular children's rhyme bandied about the schoolyard in many countries. Its origins trace back to European and African folklore, where cracks in the earth were believed to be portals to the supernatural realm, and stepping on them risked inviting unwelcome spirits into the human world.

It's rumoured that masons in the 1800s would tell this rhyme to children to encourage walking in the centre of newly paved walkways, preventing damage to the mortar before it was fully set. Perhaps this superstition is more practical than magic.

The Goodman's Croft

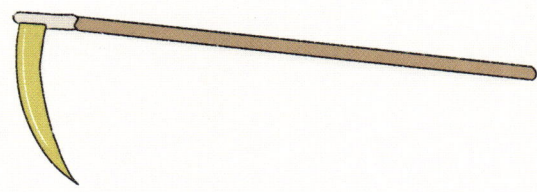

In sixteenth and seventeenth-century Britain, particularly in Scotland, a superstition known as 'The Goodman's Croft' prevailed. The practice involved setting aside a portion of cultivable land for supernatural beings; typically, a corner of a field was left untilled as an offering. People believed cultivating this land would bring bad fortune to their cattle.

By the nineteenth century, economic pressures led to the end of this practice, as crofters were forced to utilise all their available land.

Tycho Brahe Day

When it's 'just not your day', it might
be a Tycho Brahe day.

Tycho Brahe, a sixteenth-century Danish
astronomer, astrologer and alchemist, became
known as both a sage and magician. Highly
superstitious himself, he considered certain days
of the year to be especially prone to misfortune.

In Scandinavian folklore, Tycho Brahe days
are deemed particularly unlucky, especially for major
business transactions, weddings, starting journeys
or partaking in magical work. Some magical texts
even state that certain spells should not be cast
on these inauspicious days.

Umbrella Opened Indoors

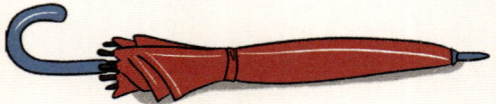

Superstition or pure pragmatism?
Whatever the weather, opening an umbrella
indoors is never a good idea.

In ancient Egypt, umbrellas were used to shade
royalty from the sun, and one theory traces umbrella
superstitions back to this practice. Opening an umbrella
indoors, away from the sun, was seen as disrespectful
and believed to anger the sun god, Ra.

Another theory from the Victorian era – when
umbrellas were big and unwieldy – was that they could
cause damage indoors; a concern that expanded
to encompass all sorts of misfortune that could
occur from opening an umbrella inside.

Unlucky Thirteen

13

Triskaidekaphobia is the fear of the number thirteen. Those who suffer from it try to avoid bad luck by steering clear of anything labelled with 'thirteen'. This superstition is so pervasive in Western cultures that it's estimated over eighty per cent of high-rise buildings in the United States don't have a thirteenth floor.

In Norse mythology, Loki – the god of mischief and disorder – was the thirteenth to arrive at a feast in Valhalla, where his presence caused a god to die during the meal. Similarly, in Christianity, Judas, who betrayed Jesus, was the thirteenth guest at the Last Supper.

With so many unlucky instances linked to thirteen, it adds up to avoid this number.

Upside-down Bread

Will this omen bring you ... *pain*?

Dating back to the Middle Ages, there's a story that French executioners would collect a loaf of bread after an execution in the town. Bakers would set aside a loaf by turning it upside down to show it was reserved for the executioner. The overturned loaf soon became associated with death and misfortune, and people avoided it for fear of casting bad luck upon themselves.

Even today, many French people believe that leaving a baguette face down could curse those who eat it with hunger or misfortune.

Walking under a Ladder

Walking under a ladder has long been considered to bring bad luck. In ancient Egypt, ladders were left in tombs for the dead to ascend with; the triangular space between the ladder and wall was said to be inhabited by spirits that shouldn't be disturbed. In medieval times, this space underneath the ladder was thought to resemble gallows, and walking through it would see you destined for the gallows yourself.

It's an enduring superstition that has changed with society over the centuries, including ways to reverse the bad luck should you step under a ladder, such as walking backwards or crossing your fingers until you see a dog. It seems that avoiding walking under a ladder might just be a step in the right direction.

Wearing Red during a Storm

In the Philippines, a superstition warns against wearing red clothing or using a red umbrella during storms, as the colour is believed to attract lightning.

While red is usually believed to be a lucky colour to wear, exuding power and energy, it's thought best to avoid in stormy weather to reduce the risk of being struck — leave the energy surges to the skies and play it safe, dressed in a colour other than red!

Yellow Flowers

A tip for a budding romance:
Think twice before giving yellow blooms.

In Russia, yellow symbolises unfaithfulness, and
it's thought that giving your lover yellow flowers will
bring bad luck or even the end of the relationship.

Additionally, it's customary to gift flowers in
odd-numbered bunches, as since ancient times in
Slavic countries, even-numbered bouquets have
been associated with mourning. Bouquets with
an even number of flowers are reserved
for funerals or placing on graves.

Yo-yo

Would you ever think the yo-yo to be a big no-no?

In 1933, a news article reported that a severe drought in Syria was killing cattle and crops. The blame fell on the recent introduction of the yo-yo, which was accused of bringing bad luck. After exposing the supposed 'evil influence' of these toys, authorities immediately banned them and police officers patrolled the streets, confiscating yo-yos from anyone caught playing with one.

With no proven outcome, belief in the yo-yo ban – like many superstitions today – simply coincided with life's many ups and downs.

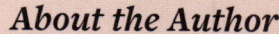

About the Author

Megan McKean is an Australian designer, author and illustrator with permanently itchy feet and a long-held curiosity for superstitions and beliefs in different cultures.

Megan's fascination with the iconography of lucky symbols has led to her collecting countless charms and souvenirs from her travels around the world.

Whether it's greeting Mr Magpie, or taking the long way around to avoid a ladder, Megan tries to stay on the lucky side of every day!

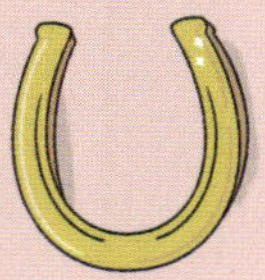

For Joshua

Still so lucky to be loving you

Published in 2025 by Hardie Grant Books, an imprint of Hardie Grant Publishing

Hardie Grant Books (Melbourne)
Wurundjeri Country
Level 11, 36 Wellington Street
Collingwood, Victoria 3066

Hardie Grant North America
2912 Telegraph Ave
Berkeley, California 94705

hardiegrant.com/books

Hardie Grant acknowledges the Traditional Custodians of the Country on which we work, the Wurundjeri People of the Kulin Nation and the Gadigal People of the Eora Nation, and recognises First Nations People's continuing connection to the land, waters and culture. We pay our respects to First Nations Elders past and present.

A catalogue record for this book is available from the National Library of Australia

Unlucky: Signs and superstitions from around the world
ISBN 978 1 76145 196 6
ISBN 978 1 76144 350 3 (ebook)

10 9 8 7 6 5 4 3 2 1

Publisher: Tahlia Anderson
Head of Editorial: Jasmin Chua
Editor: Ana Jacobsen
Creative Director: Kristin Thomas
Designer: Megan McKean
Head of Production: Todd Rechner
Production Controller: Jessica Harvie

Colour reproduction by Splitting Colour Studio
Printed in China by Leo Paper Products LTD.